The Shark who BARKED

Created by Jay Vincent and Stew Wright

Dedicated to George and any other little adventurer who has overcome huge challenges.

Your strength inspires me every day.

Down by the water in Barnacle Bay,

a boy called Ben walked his dog every day.

Ben searched in rockpools, Ted played with his ball,

when all of a sudden, they saw something small.

The closer they crept, the larger it grew,

and they spied in the sunlight that "something" was blue.

With a mouth full of teeth all gleaming and white...

A shark on a beach, an unusual sight.

"A wave must have washed him right onto the sand,

but sharks can't survive if they're stuck on dry land!"

Ted nudged the fish with his little brown snout,

who opened one eye and begged: "Please help me out!"

So the dog dug a hole to give him some traction,

while Ben gave a shove and moved him a fraction.

They pushed and they jiggled, the shark slid and wriggled,

"I'm Bluey!" he said, and his two new pals giggled.

The shark soon escaped... ***"Look Bluey, you're free!"***

said Ben to his friend, who swam out to sea

and splashed in the shallows before he returned:

"How can I repay you the favour you've earned?"

"I have many questions about the place you call home,

from coral to fishes and salty sea foam.

About whirlpools and narwhals and oh so much more.

Not much can be seen, stood here on the shore."

Bluey the shark gave a big toothy grin.

"I'd love to help out! Where shall we begin?

There's much in these waters that I still don't know,

together we'll learn what makes the sea flow."

"Do dogfish chase catfish? Do parrot fish squawk?

Do lobsters eat lunch with a knife and a fork?

Can seahorses talk? Do all sea slugs walk?

Are seashells and sand dollars made out of chalk?

How many fish are there down in the ocean?

How does a squid make its inky black potion?

Out there in the waves I see bottles afloat

with stories from pirates and curious notes...

Where is their bounty, their treasure-filled troves?

Is jelly fish ice cream a meal down below?

Do cuttle fish scuttle? Do lion fish roar?

How many shipwrecks lie on the sea floor?

I'm sure there is more that will blow my mind,

please share all the tidbits you manage to find."

So Bluey swam off to the deep ocean blue,

vowing to return with the things that he knew.

First stop was a reef, an incredible sight:

millions of fish all glistening and bright.

Eels, rays and creatures with luminous beaks...

"Parrot fish!" he cried. ***"A moment to speak?"***

"Do you chatter, do you natter or do you just squawk?

It's for my friend Ben, to whom I can talk."

But this fish was grumpy and ignored Bluey's questions,

munching **algae** instead, his preferred food ingestion.

So Bluey swam on, still enthusiastic,

but noticed the reef was covered in plastic.

Seeking the answers to tell Ben and Ted,

he spied a crustacean, both spiny and red.

"Do you use a fork when you eat your food?

I'm desperate to know, my cool shellfish dude?"

The lobster looked up... his claws made a **CLICK**.

"Don't be ridiculous, these boys do the trick!

I don't chew my meals either, no matter how yummy...

Guess where my teeth are? They live in my tummy!"

So Bluey returned with his tales from the reef,

of grumpy old fishes and tummies with teeth.

Ted BARKED with delight while Ben listened in awe.

"So much is occurring on our ocean floor!

Where will you go next and who will you see?

No Ted, there's no walkies in our open sea."

"Wait!" said Shark Bluey, ***"To ensure I don't fail...***

I need someone wiser, I need my friend...

WHALE!

"You travel afar and swim all around,

please tell me how many fish can be found?"

"Well, that's a big question and I don't really know,
but there's all sorts of species, wherever I go.

There's peculiar angler fish with crazy eyes
and lots of stone fish, hidden in disguise.

There's huge mola mola, big as the sun
and fish in my mouth, who live there for fun.

But now that you mention it, I see less these days,
they're all disappearing in mysterious ways."

And as Whale described this alarming event,

floating by were some straws, all torn up and bent.

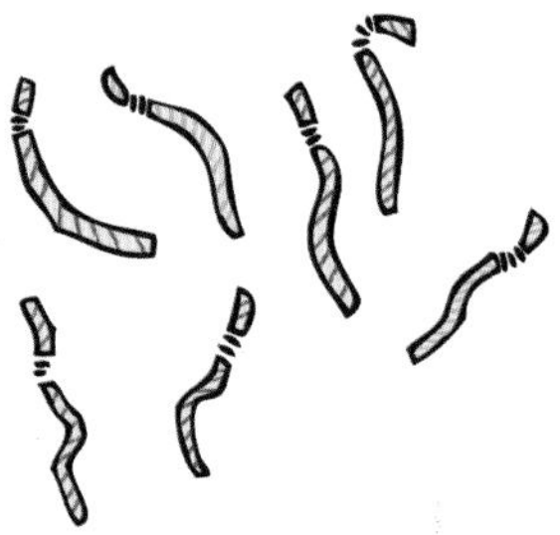

Bluey continued to seek and explore.

But what was that moving on the sea floor?

"A crab?" Bluey cried, swimming down to the sand,

but its shell had a label, now that wasn't planned.

"From the deepest sea trench to the waves on the shore,
these bottles keep coming, there's more and there's more.

As on your adventure, the oceans you roam,
can you find me a real shell, that I can call home?"

Bluey promised to find him the perfect seashell,

but as he swam back, he knew all was not well.

Fizzy

"There was a small crab with a shell made from plastic,

this problem is real, we must do something drastic!"

On hearing these tales Ben could no longer wait,

it was time to dive in and join his new mate.

A snorkel in hand, Ben jumped into the sea,

hoping that sharks wouldn't eat him for tea...

"Please tell your friends that I'm no tasty treat."

"Don't worry," said Bluey, "It's not humans we eat.

We'd rather eat sea snails, of that there's no doubt!

Sharks feel about humans as you do about SPROUTS."

They knew where to go on this leg of their quest.

To Davy Jones' locker, where pirate ships rest.

Swimming through shipwrecks from centuries before

with chests full of treasure, there's much to explore.

Ben recalled legends that came from this place!

Boats disappearing, gone without trace...

"Help!" Bluey shrieked, as he started to spin.

Ben watched in horror... what's grabbed his pal's fin?

Then all of a sudden, the whole world went black.

Were our brave friends under fishy attack?

A sound boomed out from the deep, murky drink...

"Good day," came a voice. **"You're trapped in my ink!**

I squirt all this stuff to defend what I own.

I'm extremely protective of my undersea home!"

"I'm your friend," explained Bluey. ***"I'm not your foe!***

I'll tell you our story if you just let me go."

As Bluey asked questions, Ben circled above.

How could they all save the oceans they loved?

“I’m glad that you’ve come, I’m the brain of the sea.
Even the mischievous dolphins agree.

Our life here is changing and causing us harm,
perhaps that young human can raise the alarm!”

The squid shared her knowledge with her newfound friends.

She hoped the sea’s suffering would come to an end.

Returning to shore with Ted licking his face,

Ben and Shark Bluey were straight on the case.

"We must spread the message and let the world know,

now that we realise what makes the sea flow!

There are billions of fish down there in the ocean.

But it's humans on land causing all this commotion."

"One thing is certain, no longer confused:

our magical oceans are being abused.

There's filth in the water and plastic debris,

and now overfishing is threatening the sea."

Ben shed a tear and Ted let out a "RUFF"

Bluey said quietly, ***"I think you've heard enough..."***

But they'd not seen the people all gathering behind,

who'd been listening closely to Bluey's story time.

"DID THAT GIANT FISH SPEAK?" "HE DID!" came a shout.

"THE DOG SURELY BARKED, NOT THE SHARK, THERE'S NO DOUBT!"

Bluey winked at his pals; it was his time to go.

He'd rather not star in this talking shark show!

But before he left and swam away this cheeky little shark

Splashed his tail, flashed a grin and let out an almighty...

Who knows why he barked from the ocean that day
but it got people talking in Barnacle Bay.

Bluey's story was shared, of the threat to our seas,
The giant squid's knowledge and straightforward plea:

Don't drop your litter, let's keep our seas clean.
Marine life is struggling, it's worse than it seems.

And the very last words from this fishy tale,
come from our friend, the giant blue whale...

The oceans are ours to love and to cherish.
We must all play our part to ensure they don't perish.

We hope you loved our story! Now it's your turn to learn about our oceans...

Bluey the Shark met a hermit crab who needs your help!

1. Can you find the 18 special shells hidden throughout this book?

2. What is a parrot fish's favourite food?

3. Are all lobsters red?

4. Can fish talk?

5. How much plastic enters the ocean every day?

6. How does the angler fish get its name?

7. Why can't sharks survive on dry land?

8. Which is more dangerous, a falling coconut or a shark?

9. Why are there so many bottles afloat on the ocean?

10. Why are all the fish disappearing?

11. What does the squid say we can do to protect our oceans?

12. How many different species of animal are there in the book?

Answers...

2. Algae.

3. No, the European lobster is blue. It only turns red if it's been cooked!

4. Yes, fish call out to one another to communicate.

5. We think roughly two bin lorries/garbage trucks worth of plastic enter the oceans every minute.

6. Angler fish have special bioluminescent 'lures' above their mouths that they use to attract prey – a bit like a fishing rod.

7. Most shark species need to swim constantly, so they can pass oxygen over their gills.

8. Each year, approximately 150 deaths worldwide are caused by falling coconuts, compared to only 10 deaths as a result of shark attacks!

9. People drop litter, including plastic bottles. The wind and rain wash these into the ocean, where they will take hundreds of years to break down.

10. Overfishing and plastic pollution.

11. To stop overfishing and littering and to tell everyone how the ocean needs our help.

12. 16

The Shark who BARKED

First edition printed in 2022 in the UK

ISBN: 978-1-910863-61-9

Written by: Jay Vincent

Illustrated by: Stew Wright
(www.2wrightdesign.com)

Edited by: Phil Turner, Katie Fisher

Layout by: Phil Turner, Paul Cocker

Sales and Marketing: Emma Toogood
and Lizzy Capps

mini meze

Published by Mini Meze

An imprint of Meze Publishing Limited
Unit 1B, 2 Kelham Square
Kelham Riverside
Sheffield S3 8SD
Web: www.mezepublishing.co.uk
Telephone: 0114 275 7709
Email: mini@mezepublishing.co.uk

Printed in Great Britain by Bell and Bain Ltd, Glasgow

Charity number: 1070906

The author and publisher are working closely with The Born Free Foundation to raise awareness about these key issues, with a percentage of profits going to support the charity.

Born Free work tirelessly to ensure all wild animals, whether living in captivity or the wild, are treated with compassion and respect.

Other titles in this series:

Olly is a shy but funky Orangutan, who has an incredible voice and loves to sing but can't control his nerves enough to get any words out. After falling from his perch in his favourite tree, Olly is so embarrassed, he leaves his friends and seeks sanctuary in the jungle. But will Olly discover something on his adventure that means he's finally able to overcome his fears and do what he was born to do... sing?

2020 was a year like no other, with families across the world facing the uncertainty of not seeing their families for long periods of time due to coronavirus. Written by a grandad who has not seen his grandkids for more than a year because of the pandemic, the Patch the Dog was created by Phil Vincent, who would call his grandchildren daily during lockdown and tell them of Patch's adventures over a video call.

With the help of his son, Jay, and illustrator Stew Wright, these stories have been brought to life, in a series of books to be published with one catch. Phil doesn't know it's happening.

There are 20 stories in all which formed part of Phil's daily bedtime tales, and this is the first of the 'Patch The Dog' series to be published. It tells the story of Clive The Cockerel, who's early morning crowing is causing him to fall foul of his farmyard friends, until they realise he might be the only one who can save them from disaster!